EVERYTHING I DO
YOU BLAME ON ME!

A Self-Esteem Book to Help Children Control Their Anger

By Allyson Aborn, M.S.W., C.S.W.

Illustrated by Stu Goldman

**Childswork
Childs**PLAY

Secaucus, New Jersey

EVERYTHING I DO YOU BLAME ON ME!

by Allyson Aborn, M.S.W., C.S.W.
Illustrated by Stu Goldman

Childswork/Childsplay is a catalog of products for mental health professionals, teachers, and parents who wish to help children with their developmental, social and emotional growth. For information or to obtain a catalog call toll-free 1-800-962-1141.

© 1994 Childswork/Childsplay, LLC, a subsidiary of Genesis Direct, Inc.,
100 Plaza Drive, Secaucus, NJ 07094. 1-800-962-1141.
All rights reserved.
Printed in the United States of America.

ISBN 1-882732-10-3

Helping Angry Children

Angry children can be the bane of their parents' existence and their teacher's worst nightmare. They can be defiant, aggressive, and perpetually unhappy. The reasons for their anger are sometimes apparent. They be may be reacting to a divorce, a family move, a new sibling in the home, or rejection by their peers. They may come from an "angry" family, where parents fight excessively, or a family where people take their anger out on the child.

But for all these obvious scenarios, there are just as many situations where it is not apparent why a child is angry or aggressive. In spite of their parents' and teacher's love and concern, these children may have frequent outbursts, tantrums, or act in surprisingly anti-social ways.

No matter what the cause, angry children need to learn self-control and the socially-appropriate behaviors that will break the pattern of rejection and disappointment.

In the first part of this "double book," children follow the progress of a boy named Eddie and learn some of the most effective techniques available to help children control and transform their anger. In the second book, children can practice their own decision-making skills as they choose their own resolutions to the conflicts experienced by a boy having common difficulties with his family.

There are no simple solutions to helping angry children. Working with them takes patience and perseverance. We hope that this book will serve as a "jumping off" spot in considering some of the alternatives to be explored in the treatment of these children.

1

Hi. This is me, Eddie. You can call me Eddie. Or you can call me by my new name, invented by my dad. My dad calls me "Steady Eddie."

This is the story of how I got my new name. It might be a story you've never heard before. Or, when I'm telling you the story, you might say, "Hey, this guy Eddie is just like Nicole, or Sam, or Becca, or Ben."

You can put another kid's name into the story instead of mine, if you want. It's that kind of book. You can see whether the things that happened to me are like the things that happen to you or someone you know.

You're going to be able to choose other things, too. After I tell you about what happened to me, you can turn this book *upside down* and read a story where *you* decide what will happen.

You'll see.

As I told you, my name wasn't always Steady Eddie. For the first seven years of my life, I thought my name was CUT IT OUT, EDDIE!

7

At home, at least a hundred times a day, my mom would yell, over and over, "CUT IT OUT, EDDIE!" At school, my teachers would say, over and over, "CUT IT OUT, EDDIE!" Ditto my brother and my sister and my soccer coach and all my *ex-best* friends. (I have a lot of those).

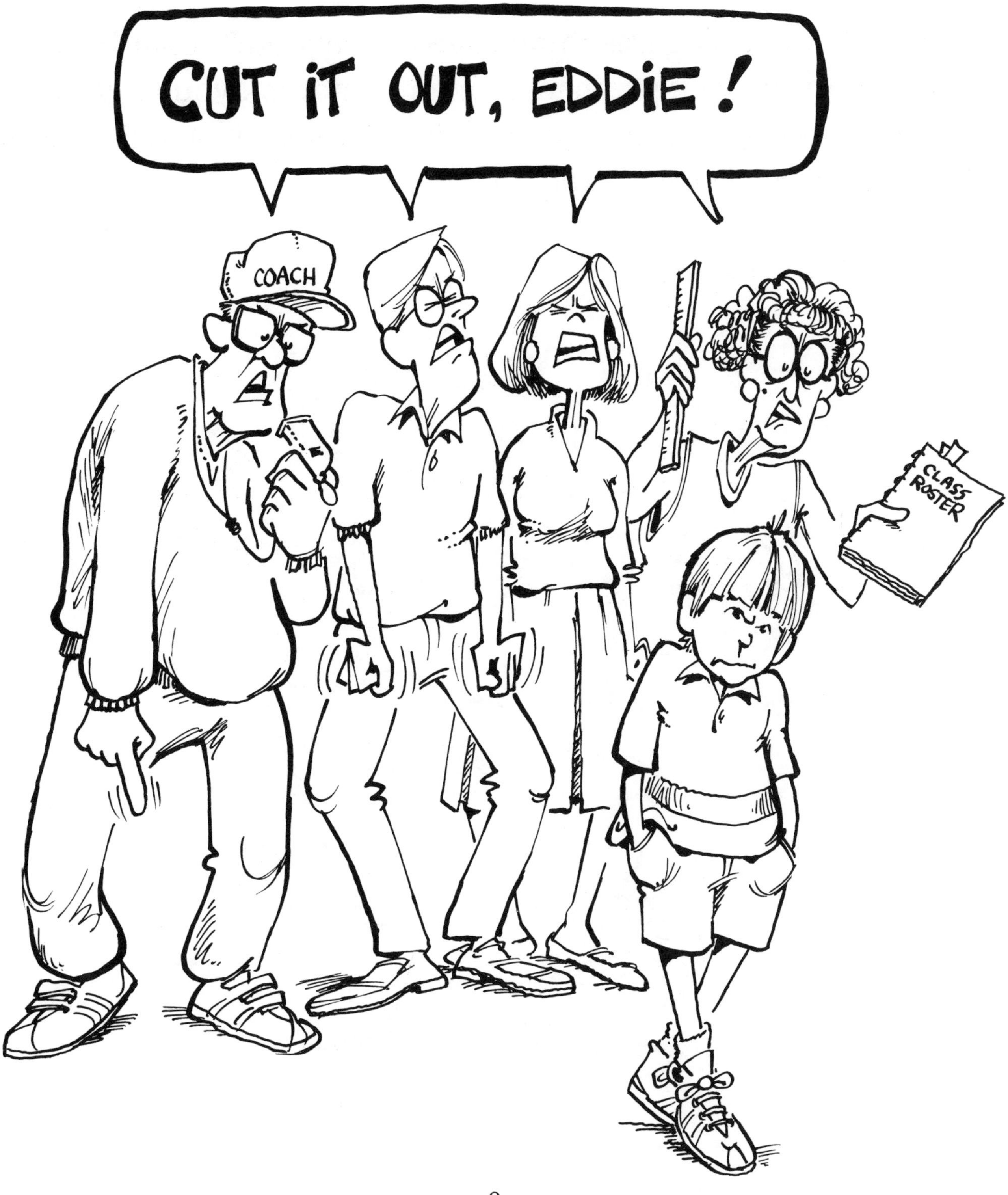
CUT IT OUT, EDDIE!
COACH
CLASS ROSTER

I was always doing this thing called "going off." Ever hear of that? It means you get mad, *so* mad, you think you're going to explode. Well, that's not quite right. Because what happens is that you *don't do the thinking part.*

All you do *is* explode.

WHAM!! BAM!! WHACK!! SMASH!! All day long I was mad about *everything*. *Everything* bugged me. *Everybody* bugged me. *Everything I did I got blamed for!*

I'm going to tell you about the day I started to make the change from CUT IT OUT, EDDIE! to Steady Eddie. Then I'll tell you about what I have to do to *stay* Steady Eddie.

Because every day is still hard.

There are still times *every single day* that CUT IT OUT, EDDIE! wants to get his way.

This is my room. I share it with my brother, Billy The Pest.

We used to fight every single second.

Now we still fight, but not as much and not as mean.

On this one morning, I woke up and saw Billy playing with my third best racing car. I jumped from my bed onto his and smacked him, hard. He smacked me back and we were shouting and hitting and Mom came running in and pulled us apart.

She was always taking Billy's side and being gooey-nice to him. That day, she even helped him get dressed.

I couldn't find my favorite blue tee shirt, so I threw all the stuff out of my drawers looking for it.

"CUT IT OUT, EDDIE!" she screamed.

When we finally made it to breakfast, Billy said, "You're so stupid you can't even pour your cereal right."

I hit his bowl as hard as I could with my spoon and his cereal went flying around the room like a tornado.

"CUT IT OUT, EDDIE!" Mom shrieked again.

I screeched back my chair just the way she hates it, grabbed my backpack, and ran out of the kitchen. The dumb old door stuck, so I kicked it. That's nothing new. There are marks and chips all over the door where I've kicked to get it open. There are chips in a lot of walls in the house, too. Dad didn't even bother patching them. He said, "Everyone might as well see what a lousy kid you are."

19

I got to the bus stop just as the bus pulled up. I could tell all the kids were watching me and talking about me. Boy, do I hate that.

"Eddie is a dwee-eeb, Eddie is a cree-eep," they started chanting. I threw down my pack. Andrew was closest to me so I grabbed his arm and twisted it. No one was going to mess with me.

The bus monitor raced down the steps. "CUT IT OUT, EDDIE!" she yelled, and pulled Andrew away.

On the bus the kids kept teasing me and I kicked at everyone I could reach. I hated that bus! I hated those kids! I hated everything!

By the time I got to my classroom, my jeans were covered with sneaker marks and my lunch bag was ripped. Right away Mr. Caruso, my teacher, gave us a timed test on the multiplication tables. I couldn't remember hardly any of them. That made me so mad! I crumpled my paper into a little ball and threw it as hard as I could at the back of Michael's head.

Mr. Caruso came over to my desk. Very softly, he said, "You have 90 seconds left; let's try to stay steady and finish the test."

I smashed my books off my desk onto the floor.

Then I started to cry.

The other kids were laughing at me.

"Eddie, that's it," Mr. Caruso said. "You're going to Dr. Reed. Now."

This was nothing new, either. I was going to Dr. Reed every single day.

I would sit outside her office until I calmed down. Then we would talk about how I needed to control myself better.

I tried to tell her why I was so mad and how it was not my fault, but this day was different. This day, when I went in, Dr. Reed said, "Eddie, Mr. Caruso and I have tried every way we can to help you stay steady. We are out of ideas. I have called both your mother and your father. They are coming in right now to talk so we can figure out together what to do."

Now I was really mad. And scared. Why did she have to call my dad? My mom says my dad has a "short fuse." When he gets mad, watch out. He yells and he curses. He shouts at my mom that she can't handle me.

Sometimes he even pops me one. One time he threw a wooden spoon at me and got me in the back of the leg. They should have been meeting about *him*, not me.

That day, Dr. Reed and Mr. Caruso and my parents talked for a long time. Then they called me in.

Dr. Reed said, "We all want to help you to get along better at home and at school and with other kids. We know it is hard for you to control yourself. We are going to send you to a special children's doctor who will help you to learn how to do that."

NO WAY!! I crashed the chair against Dr. Reed's desk. I yelled. I cursed, too. (But I can't say those words now).

GUESS WHAT? My mom and dad took me anyway. Kicking and screaming. Dad *carried me* from the car, into the doctor's office.

Dr. Bruce

The first couple of weeks, I wouldn't even talk to Dr. Bruce. I was too busy trashing his office. He didn't get mad at me, he just said he wouldn't let me hurt myself or him and I had to clean up everything I messed.

After a while, it wasn't so much fun doing scribblescrabble on his walls when I had to scrub them clean before I could leave. *And* he made me scrub another wall, too, that I didn't even draw on.

One day when I was really mad, Dr. Bruce said, "Why not give that punching bag a try?"

So I did. Boy, did I start to love that bag. Sometimes I'd go to Dr. Bruce's and hit it for the whole session. While I was smacking it around, Dr. Bruce would talk to me.

"All kids are born different," he told me. "Some are quiet and like to sit around doing puzzles. Others can't sit still, and need to climb and run and explore everything. Some kids are picky eaters. Some kids are scared of the dark. Different things are hard for different kids.

"It's hard for you to control your temper. Maybe you were just born that way. Maybe there are other people in your family who had trouble controlling themselves too, and you 'inherited' that, just like you inherited your freckles and brown eyes. Or, maybe you have been around people who have trouble controlling themselves too."

I thought of my dad when he said that.

"You and I are going to figure out better ways for you to handle your angry feelings, so that you do not hurt yourself or other people, and so that you can feel happier."

Yeah, right, I thought.

Dr. Bruce said, "Stop punching for a minute and come over here by the light. Open your mouth. Stick out your tongue."

He looked right in my mouth for a long time.

Then he said, "Eddie, do you know what I saw in there?" I shook my head.

"You have *words* in there, loads and loads of them. We can learn how you can use those words instead of punches and kicks, to get what you want. Those words have super-powers that your fists and feet will never have. Will you give this a try?"

He put out his hand. Slowly, I put out mine. We shook. "Partners," he said. I didn't say anything.

We got down to work. The first thing Dr. Bruce did was to make a "Behavior Chart" for me. He talked to my parents and my teacher, and we decided together what would be on my school chart and on my home chart. This is what my first home chart said:

Eddie will keep his hands to himself
Eddie will come in from playing when Mom calls
Eddie will use good language
Eddie will go to bed on time
Eddie will tell Mom or Dad if he and Billy are having trouble

	MON	TUE	WED	THU	FRI	SAT	SUN
Eddie will keep his hands to himself							
Eddie will come in from playing when Mom calls							
Eddie will use good language							
Eddie will go to bed on time							
Eddie will tell Mom or Dad if he and Billy are having trouble							

When I followed what the chart said, I earned a sticker. When I had 15 stickers on my chart, I could win a prize! When I earned 21 I could win an even bigger prize! I could win a pack of Superhero cards!

MON
TUE
WED
THU
FRI
SAT
SUN
Eddie will keep his hands to himself
Eddie will come in from playing when Mom calls
Eddie will use good language
Eddie will go to bed on time
Eddie will tell Mom or Dad if he and Billy are having trouble

At first I was all excited. Piece of cake, I thought. The problem was, I couldn't seem to win any stickers. Why? I wasn't used to controlling myself. IT WAS SO HARD!!!

But Dr. Bruce wouldn't give up. Every week I'd bring him a chart with two or three stickers and he would say, "I know this is hard for you, but look, you did it here," and he would point to one puny sticker. "I know you can do it. Let's try again."

He started me out on another plan, too. It was called "Time Out." Some of you may have heard about that. It means you have to sit quietly and all alone sometimes until you get steady again.

My mom and dad had tried "Time Out" a long time ago, when I was in nursery school, but they gave up on it when I gave them such a hard time, even though they did it *because* I was giving them a hard time.

Dr. Bruce said there were certain things I could not do, no matter what. This is the list we started with:

NO saying bad words!
NO hitting!
NO biting!
NO kicking!
NO throwing things!

Dr. Bruce made *100* copies of these rules. He said, "Put these all over your room so that you see them everywhere you look. Put them on the ceiling over your bed so that you see them first thing when you wake up every morning."

I thought that was pretty strange, but I did it anyway.

When I broke a rule, I had to do a "time-out." Mom put an old porch chair in the corner of the dining room, where it is always quiet. She called it the "Time-Out Chair." She put a cooking timer on the table near the chair.

When I broke a rule, she set the timer and I had to sit quietly in the chair and get myself steady. She would never set the timer for longer than how old I was.

When Dr. Bruce told my mom about "time out," she said, "It *sounds* easy enough," and she looked me in the eyes and lowered her eyebrows. I guess she had good reason to look funny at me.

Most times, especially at the beginning, I plain old wouldn't do my time out. I'd yell and kick and punch.

Then Mom would say, "Dr. Bruce told me if you wouldn't cooperate with me, I should 'time-out' something else, something that you like."

So she would "time-out" things like video games or my new baseball mitt, or my bike, which meant they were taken away, sometimes for a day or more.

Little by little, I started working harder at trying to calm myself down so I could do my time-out and not lose my stuff.

When I saw Dr. Bruce we would sometimes make up little stories and act them out. We would think up a problem. Like once, the problem was that a big kid took my backpack and ran around the playground with it.

First Dr. Bruce pretended he was the big kid. I started chasing after him with a pretend bat. I'd show him. Dr. Bruce said, "STOP! Let's imagine what could happen if you chase a big kid with a bat."

"He'll smack me back," I said.

"Then what?"

"Then the playground monitor will see me chasing him and send me to the principal," I said.

"Then what?" Dr. Bruce asked again.

"Then the principal will call my parents and suspend me again," I replied.

"Let's play the game again," Dr. Bruce suggested. "This time I'll be the big kid and you be you. And we're going to think up other ways for you to get your pack back without you getting into trouble."

This was tough. I couldn't come up with one idea at first. But Dr. Bruce helped me out, until I had the hang of it.

He said, "Pretend you are a turtle. Stick your arms and legs and head into your shell. While you are in there, figure out what you can do about this problem. When you are ready, *then* come out."

I tried it, lots of times. Finally, when I came out of my shell, I said, "I could *ask* the boy to put down my pack. *Or*, I could ignore him and ask the kids I was playing with to ignore him, too. If he saw no one was paying attention to what he was doing maybe he would just drop my pack. *Or*, I could go to the playground monitor and ask her to help me get my pack back."

"GREAT SHELL WORK!" Dr. Bruce applauded. He said we were "exploring my choices." It was kind of fun.

And when I tried it out with real problems, IT WORKED!

Dr. Bruce said that I was doing much better at controlling my anger, but I was still having trouble. When I was *really mad*, I didn't have time to think about choices. I would still kick or curse or hit before I even knew I did it. So Dr. Bruce started teaching me how to relax.

"This will help you a lot to get steady, Eddie," he said. Dr. Bruce told me that as soon as I started feeling mad, I should take a big long breath, and I should let it out V-E-R-Y S-L-O-W-L-Y, like I was blowing bubbles. We even went to the toy store and bought a special bubble pipe. The slower you blew, the bigger the bubble.

Then he taught me how to count V-E-R-Y S-L-O-W-L-Y, like this:

ONE - I'M STEADY - TWO - I'M STEADY...All the way up to TEN - I'M READY.

He taught me how to sit down and pretend I was a big, floppy rag doll, all loose and wobbly. We'd sit on Dr. Bruce's couch and get all relaxed.

Dr. Bruce also taught me how to relax by using my imagination. I would get all rag-doll comfortable in his big black chair and then I would imagine that I was in some really neat quiet place. It was like making my own home video, and playing it back inside my head.

I imagined I was floating along on a big raft in the middle of the lake near where Grampa lives. I looked up and saw puffy clouds and I could feel the raft rocking a little bit in the water. I felt so good...I felt quiet.

Still, it was hard to remember all the stuff I was practicing with Dr. Bruce when I was really mad. That made me mad: mad at myself, and mad at other people for making me mad.

Dr. Bruce had an idea for this, too.

Dr. Bruce pretended he was me. He pretended he had a spelling test at school and he couldn't remember the hard words. "This is stupid!" he yelled, and he tore the pretend test into pieces and let it snow down on us.

I laughed. He looked so dumb. He spun around and made a mean face, with his eyes scrunched up and his hands in fists. "You want to go for it?" he threatened. All of a sudden I felt afraid. I curled up into the corner of the couch.

Dr. Bruce put down his fists and turned back into his regular self. "See, Eddie, that is how you look to other people sometimes. What do you think?"

"You looked stupid and scary at the same time," I whispered. "I wouldn't want to be friends with you."

That was when Dr. Bruce taught me how to talk to myself.

Yup. Talk to myself.

Dr. Bruce pretended he was me again. I was the teacher, handing him the test.

He looked at the test. Then he spoke softly to himself.

"OK, now what is it I have to do? I have to figure out which words are spelled right and which are not. I have to look at each letter and take my time. The first word is 'believe.' 'I before E except after C.' So this is spelled right. Good. I did this one.

"Now I'll have a look at the next one. Uh-oh. I don't have a clue how to spell this one. Remember not to race through. Go slowly to the next word and then come back to this word. You are doing a good job."

Dr. Bruce said, "You see how I can coach myself through a problem? It's like when your soccer coach keeps saying to you, 'Keep your eye on the ball' or 'Kick with your whole leg.' And then when you set up the ball for a kick, *you say these things to yourself.*

"You can even do this when you're angry. You can coach yourself just like I coach you in my office."

It took me a long time to get used to this. At first I had to talk out loud to myself. Now, most of the time, I can talk to myself inside my head. I have my own helper and my helper is *me*.

You're probably wondering, does all this stuff I've told you about really work? Well, sometimes it works better than others.

Let me tell you about the last big problem day that I've had in a long, long time.

It was the nicest day of the year. Sunny and warm. Everyone was playing down the street. Then Mom called me to come in first of *all the kids on the block.*

I didn't remember to take slow breaths or count or talk to myself. I was so mad! I kicked a new hole in the screen door.

"CUT IT OUT, EDDIE!" she screamed, same as always. But then, instead of screaming, she got her regular voice back, and she said, "You need to do a time-out." She took my arm and walked me to the time-out chair and set the timer. I chased after her, yelling and grabbing at her. I don't know why, but she stayed calm.

"Get steady, Eddie," she said, and she marched me back to the chair. She reset the timer for the whole time. That got me even madder. This time I leaped out of the chair, crashing it down.

"Pick up the chair and get steady, Eddie," Mom said again, calm as anything.

"NO! NO! NO! NO! NO! NO! NO! NO! NO! NO!"

We went at it like this forever. Mom didn't raise her voice, not even once. She just kept telling me I had to do my time-out.

Finally, I was so tired, I just picked up the chair and sat in it and she set the timer and left the room.

That night I didn't get any stickers on my chart. Which meant I didn't have enough stickers for the week to earn the glow-in-the-dark superhero cards I wanted more than anything in the world.

From that night on, I started trying harder. What helped most was that it seemed like it wasn't just me who was trying. My mom was really trying, too. And my dad, too.

Driving home from Little League one day, Dad said, "Sometimes I let myself be too mad at you. How can I expect you to control yourself when I don't control myself? Mom and I have been learning how to control ourselves better in Dr. Bruce's parents group. We want to do better, too."

Then, when the light turned red, Dad leaned over and gave me a big hug. He looked like he was about to cry. I wasn't sad, I was happy, but I felt like I wanted to cry, too.

So, that's how it is right now. I still go to Dr. Bruce. Now we don't have to practice "tricks" so much. Now we spend most of our time talking about what makes me so mad and why. He helps me figure stuff out. The more I figure out, the less mad I become.

I still do my charts and have time-outs, but not so many, and more and more I can stop myself from being wild before I have to do a time-out.

In school, I try to relax and to talk to myself. Mr. Caruso and Dr. Reed both say how proud they are that I don't (hardly ever) hit and kick and throw things and curse. They help me out, just like Mom and Dad do at home.

The best part of all this is about the other kids. Now that I'm not punching out their lights every minute, they are letting me hang out with them more and more. Last week, I was the fourth one picked, not the very last one, in the kickball game down the street.

Well, that's my story. Now it's your turn. So turn this book over and let's see how you will do, getting through a day.

GOOD LUCK!!!

About the Author:

Allyson Aborn, M.S.W., C.S.W. is an expert in the fields of child development and family therapy. She maintains a private practice in Scarsdale, NY specializing in the treatment of children, families and couples. Ms. Aborn is on staff in the Outpatient Department at New York Hospital/Cornell Medical Center, and has served for many years as a consultant at a therapeutic nursery school. Ms. Aborn has written extensively in the field of child psychiatry. Her first book, Hooray for Henry! *was published in 1990. She is the author of a chapter in* The Therapeutic Powers of Play *(1993), edited by Charles E. Schaefer, Ph.D. Her articles have appeared in* The New York Times *and she is co-author of a screen adaptation of an Anne Tyler novel. She is the mother of three children.*

About the Illustrator:

Stu Goldman, in addition to illustrating, is an internationally-syndicated political cartoonist, actor and teacher. He lives and works in Philadelphia, Pennsylvania.

About the Self-Esteem Series:

Self-esteem is more than just liking oneself. It is a deep and overriding sense of self-worth and well-being, which comes from a realistic sense of competency and success in the world. But how can this be achieved with children who are characterized as "problem" children? The Self-Esteem Series addresses the challenges of children who are "different" and offers solutions in helping them develop a positive self-image.

WHY <u>SHOULD</u> I? IT'S NOT <u>MY</u> BIRTHDAY!

A CHOOSE-YOUR-OWN-SOLUTION BOOK

By Allyson Aborn, M.S.W., C.S.W.

Childswork ChildsPLAY

Secaucus, New Jersey

The kid in this book is angry—angry at his mom, angry at his little brother, angry that everyone is making such a fuss about his brother's birthday—and he's not sure what he should do about his anger. You have the chance to help him decide.

Most books tell you what happens to the characters in the story. This book is different—you can decide what will happen on each page. Just choose what you want to happen, and if you want, you can change the ending each time you read the story!

You might recognize the main character in this book. He might remind you of someone you know, or he might be a lot like you. In any case, we hope you have some fun with this book as you help him decide what to do.

When you wake up, the sky is still a tiny bit dark. You know this is going to be a BIG DAY!!! Your brother Andy's birthday party is at noon, and then, right after that is the playoff soccer match against the Townline Tigers!

You can't stay in bed, not when you're feeling so wiggly. You peek into Mom's room; she's still asleep. So is Andy. So are Lucy and Ducy, the cats. You pull each of their tails to see what will happen. Sure enough, they wake up. Lucy gives you a look and rolls over, and Ducy hisses.

You notice that Mom has loaded the dining room table with lots of party stuff: candy, little toys for the goody bags, balloons, paper streamers. Why? She didn't buy that much for your party. In fact, only four kids came to your party. Everyone else said "no" to the invitation.

If you decide to wake Mom and ask her if you can start decorating on your own, turn to page 2.

If you decide to surprise Mom by getting everything ready for the party, turn to page 3.

If you feel really angry when you see what Mom has done for Andy's party, turn to page 5.

You jump hard on Mom's bed.

"Stop it!" she yells.

"I'm gonna get everything ready for the party," you tell her.

"No, you're not!"

"Am so!"

"NO!"

You run out of the room.

If you return to the dining room, turn to page 3.

If you return to your room, turn to page 7.

There's so much stuff on the table, you don't know what to do first. You rip open the balloon bag and try blowing one up. You can't do it. You throw it aside and try another. And another.

You are feeling more frustrated. You decide to start making the goody bags, but you are confused by what to put in each one, and you keep forgetting which ones you've already finished. Now you are feeling mad.

You start cursing, loud. Your mom walks in.

"What do you think you're doing?!" she shouts.

If you try to get steady, turn to page 4.

If seeing your mom makes you even madder, turn to page 6.

You look up at your mom. She puts her hands on your shoulders. Then you remember to pretend you are a turtle, pulling yourself into your shell until you can figure out what to do about the mess you've made.

You count slowly to yourself, and between each number, you pretend you are blowing out a birthday candle.

If you are beginning to feel more relaxed, turn to page 8.

If you just can't slow yourself down and you try to break away from your mom, turn to page 9.

You start throwing things off the table and ripping up the streamers.

Your mom runs into the room and sees what you are doing.

"You need a time-out," she says.

Turn to page 9.

"You need to do a time-out," your mom tells you.

If you are able to do the time-out, turn to page 8.

If you can't calm down enough to do the time-out, turn to page 7.

You run into your room and slam the door. You feel like smashing every toy on the shelves. Instead, you make the choice to try the relaxing tricks you've been working on.

You open the bottle of bubbles behind your bed. You take a deep breath in, then you breathe out slowly, forming an enormous bubble. You keep blowing bubbles until you feel quieter.

Then you lie down on your bed and slip an imaginary video into the pretend VCR in your head. You imagine you are at the beach, and the sand and the sun feel all nice and warm. You can hear the waves and you can also hear the sound of the bell on the ice cream truck.

Your mom walks in.

Turn to page 8.

"I am so proud of you. You kept yourself steady," your mom says.

She gives you a big hug. "How about being my special party helper?" she asks you. "ALL RIGHT!!!"

Turn to page 10.

"Leave me alone!" you shout.

"Time to do a time-out," your mom says firmly.

"NO WAY!!!"

You throw the goody bags on the floor. Your mom takes you by the arm and plops you down in the time-out chair.

"You need to get steady," she states again. "If you can't get steady you can't help me with the party."

You kick her hard in the leg.

Your mom says, "You just lost the chance to help me. Go to your room."

It is an hour before you are calm enough to do your time-out.

Your mom sticks to her word and doesn't let you prepare for the party with her and Andy.

If you are steady enough to be at the party, turn to page 10.

The kids begin to arrive for Andy's party. Lots of kids. With lots of presents. All for Andy. Everyone is running around and talking and yelling. It's so exciting, you don't know what to do first.

Then Jimmy, the meanest kid in the whole school, slinks toward you. He looks around to see that no grown-ups are near.

"Hey, pea brain, who let you out of your cage?" he growls in a low voice only you can hear.

"Leave me alone," you answer, clenching and unclenching your fists.

"You wanna make me, you little wimp?" He moves closer, and steps hard on your foot.

If you punch Jimmy in the gut, turn to page 11.

If you turn your back on him, turn to page 12.

Jimmy rams you into the wall. You crash into the table where the birthday cake is set up.

Suddenly, everyone at the party is shouting and pushing. Your dad's arm appears out of nowhere. You didn't even realize he had arrived at the party. He drags you out of the scuffle.

He pulls you into your room.

"You just wrecked your brother's birthday, " he yells. "You can spend the rest of the party in here," he adds, and slams the door shut.

You miss the cake and the presents and the games.

Turn to page 13.

You run into your room. You know you need to calm down. You begin to count.

"One - I'm steady - Two - I'm steady - Three - I'm steady..."

Your mom enters.

"I saw what happened with Jimmy," she tells you. "You did a great job of controlling yourself. As soon as you feel steady enough, come back out. I called Jimmy's mom and told her to take him home. You can be in charge of putting the candles on the cake."

Turn to page 13.

The party is finally over. You leave with your dad for the soccer field, where the playoff is beginning.

Your coach doesn't play you much in the first half. Now it is the third quarter. When you remind him again that you want to go in, he says, "Be ready; any second now."

Still, the waiting is hard. You kick the bench. The coach sees you.

"Watch it," he warns. Then he makes you wait until the fourth quarter before he puts you in.

Turn to page 14.

Now you are running down the field. There are three minutes left in the fourth quarter. A player from the Townline Tigers cuts you off and elbows you hard. He steals the ball away.

If you push the other player back really hard, turn to page 16.

If you curse the other player out, turn to page 16.

If you raise your arm for the referee to stop the play, turn to page 17.

If you keep on playing and say to yourself, "I am playing really well. I am a good player and I can help my team to win," turn to page 15.

You keep talking to yourself and paying attention to the game. When the ball comes your way again, you are ready for it. You pass to the center forward, who makes the shot.

"Great play!!!" your teammates shout.

Turn to page 19.

You knock the other player down and call him a terrible name. You get thrown out of the game. Your team has to play the rest of the game with one less player. Your teammates are very angry with you.

Turn to page 18.

The referee sees your hand and stops the play. He talks to you to ask what happened and then he talks to the linesman. Your team gets a corner kick and scores a goal. The other kids surround you and give you a "2-4-6-8 Who-Do-We-Appreciate" cheer.

Turn to page 19.

You feel really bad. When you arrive home from soccer, the place is still a mess from the party.

Your mom makes you go to bed early. When she comes to tuck you in, she says, "I'm sorry you didn't try harder today. Let's both try harder tomorrow. Deal?"

You nod your head.

She gives you a long snuggle. Then she turns out the big light and turns on the night light.

"Good night."

"Night."

THE END

After the game, the whole team goes out for pizza. You have a great time. The team gives the coach a new whistle with "SUPERCOACH" engraved on it.

The coach stands up. The room grows quiet.

"It's been a great season," he says. "You guys really played like a team. You deserved to win today."

Then he turns to you.

"And here's a special cheer for our special halfback—you made it happen today!"

You look over at your dad. He gives you the "two thumbs up" sign and a great big smile.

"YES!!!"

THE END